This Storybook Belongs to:

Princess _____

Jasmine

Star Bright

Advance
PUBLISHERS

Aladdin held out his hand and helped Princess Jasmine onto the waiting Magic Carpet. "Where would you like to go tonight?" he asked. "Your wish is my command."

"It doesn't matter," Jasmine replied. "As long as we're together, I know it will be a wonderful evening."

"All right, then," said Aladdin. "We'll let the Magic Carpet decide!"

They lifted off the balcony of the palace and gently glided up, up, up into the sky.

"Look over there!" Jasmine exclaimed suddenly. "It's a violet star!"

"That's the Star of Dorri," Aladdin explained. "It was named after a beautiful queen who was known for her exceptional kindness to her people. She was also famous for the magnificent purple amethyst that graced her headpiece. After she died, a violet star appeared in the sky. Her subjects believed the star was her spirit watching over them. A generation later, the people of that kingdom still believe it."

"What happened to her headpiece?" Jasmine wondered.

"It is locked in a tower in the royal palace," replied Aladdin, "and only those who prove themselves worthy are allowed to see it."

"Where is this kingdom?" Jasmine asked.

"Far, far away from Agrabah," said Aladdin. "Why? You're not thinking of going there, are you?" But he already knew the answer when he saw the twinkle in Jasmine's eyes.

"Why not?" she challenged. "Nothing is that far away when you have a Magic Carpet to take you there! Wouldn't you like to see Queen Dorri's amethyst, too?"

"Do I have a choice?" Aladdin asked with a smile.

"Not really," replied the Princess.

And so the Magic Carpet flew all through the night and into the next morning. Abu was certainly surprised to awake from his nap in Aladdin's cape to find them all heading toward an imposing palace!

"That must be Queen Dorri's royal compound!" Jasmine cried. "It's magnificent!"

"Look at that tower! I've never seen a building so tall!" declared Aladdin. "It's obvious that the people of this kingdom don't want anyone getting close to Queen Dorri's headpiece."

Abu chattered and pointed to the door of the tower. "And Abu doesn't like the look of that guard—or his axe," Aladdin said.

"Listen to the two of you!" scolded Jasmine. "Honestly, I'm sure once I talk to the guard, he'll let us in to see the gem in no time."

Jasmine strolled over to the burly sentry and gave him her most charming smile.

"Good day," she began. "My name is Princess Jasmine. Tales of your Queen Dorri have reached my kingdom in Agrabah, and I have traveled far to pay tribute to her. Please, may I have the honor of entering the tower so that I may view the headpiece your queen wore during her magnificent reign?"

"No!" the guard said gruffly. "No one is worthy to see Queen Dorri's jewel. No one!"

"Oh dear," thought Jasmine, "this is going to be more difficult than I imagined."

"Oh, but kind sir," said Aladdin, stepping forward. "I'm sure if you got to know Princess Jasmine, you would change your mind. She is beloved by all in Agrabah."

"This is not Agrabah!" barked the guard. "Your princess cannot possibly be as smart, fair-minded, or kindhearted as our Queen Dorri was."

Princess Jasmine stood a little straighter. She loved a challenge! "Why not put me to a test and see for yourself?" she asked.

The guard considered this for a moment. "Our queen was a gifted mathematician," he declared. "For example, if were to you ask her, 'What is the square root of 100?' instantly she would answer —"

"Ten," interrupted Jasmine.

$$\sqrt{100} = 10$$

"Impressive," mumbled the guard, but he was soon distracted by an argument taking place across the road.

"You see that?" he asked.

"When Queen Dorri was alive, the marketplace was filled with the sounds of friendship, not conflict."

Jasmine strode over to the two arguing men. "Excuse me," she said, "what seems to be the problem?"

"My neighbor and I agreed to a trade," said one of the men, "but look how small his fish is compared to my fowl! He is surely getting the bigger meal!"

"Why don't you have dinner together, and share both between you?" Jasmine suggested. "You'll have plenty of food and good company, too!"

"What a splendid idea!" the friends agreed. Soon they were laughing and slapping each other on the back.

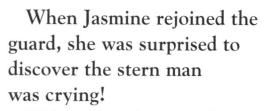

When Jasmine rejoined the guard, she was surprised to discover the stern man was crying!

"Oh my goodness! What's wrong?" she asked.

"I can't help it," the guard said through his tears. "I must admit that you do remind me a bit of Queen Dorri. Life in our kingdom just hasn't been the same since she's been gone. It's as if all of our joy left with her."

"You poor man," soothed Jasmine. "Let me get you a cool drink of water."

Jasmine sat on the edge of a fountain and filled a jar with water. By now she had forgotten all about Queen Dorri's headpiece. All she could think about was what the guard had told her.

I've got to help these people learn to be happy again, Jasmine thought.

Suddenly, Jasmine sensed she was being watched. She turned to see a throng of townspeople gathered around the fountain, all staring at her with an astonished expression.

"You filled it with water!" exclaimed the guard.

"I'm sorry," Jasmine said. "Did I use a jar I wasn't supposed to?"

"No, you don't understand," he continued. "On the day our queen passed, that fountain dried up. It hasn't given us a drop of water since . . . until today!"

"It's a miracle!" someone shouted.

"It's a sign!" cried another. "Queen Dorri has sent her to us!"

A murmur went through the crowd, and seconds later the entire crowd bowed before Jasmine.

"Hail to our new queen!" declared the guard. He reverently approached Jasmine and held out the key to the tower.

Jasmine held up her hands. "I think there has been a mistake," she said gently. "The spirit of Queen Dorri may very well have sent me to you, but I am not meant to be your queen. My duty is to my own kingdom of Agrabah. But I do believe I am here to remind you that even though your queen has died, your joy in life should remain alive."

"Thank you for bringing this message from our queen," replied the guard. "I know she would want to thank you by making you a gift of her most prized possession. Please, follow me."

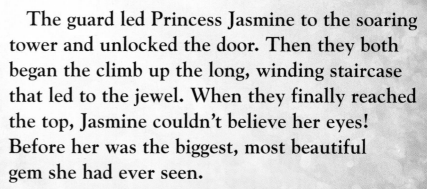

The guard led Princess Jasmine to the soaring
tower and unlocked the door. Then they both
began the climb up the long, winding staircase
that led to the jewel. When they finally reached
the top, Jasmine couldn't believe her eyes!
Before her was the biggest, most beautiful
gem she had ever seen.

"It's magnificent," Jasmine whispered.

"Just like our queen," added the guard.

He removed the headpiece from its pedestal and held it up for Princess Jasmine to have a closer look.

"I've never seen a jewel glow like this before," said Princess Jasmine. "Do beams of light always radiate from it like this?"

"Only when the spirit of Queen Dorri is especially happy," the guard answered. "I believe she is pleased that the jewel is going to be worn again. Go ahead, put it on."

When Jasmine emerged from the tower, she had an announcement to make. "I am honored that you have offered me your beloved queen's amethyst," she began, "but I believe the jewel rightly belongs to you, her people. I will only borrow it for a time, so that I may bring it to distant lands and share with others tales of Queen Dorri's many kindnesses. I promise to treat her gem—and her memory—with the utmost care."

Then she, Aladdin, and Abu bid their new friends good-bye and set off on their journey.

That night, as Jasmine looked up into the sky, she couldn't help but notice that the Star of Dorri seemed to be sparkling more brightly than ever before.